MORE
GROSS

MORE GROSS

CARTOONS BY

S.GROSS

 CONGDON & WEED · NEW YORK

Copyright © 1982 by S. Gross

Distributor's ISBN: 0-312-92540-9

Publisher's ISBN: 0-86553-057-2

Library of Congress Catalog Card Number: 82-73194

Published by Congdon & Weed, Inc.

298 Fifth Avenue, New York, N.Y. 10001

Distributed by St. Martin's Press

175 Fifth Avenue, New York, N.Y. 10010

Published simultaneously in Canada by Thomas Nelson & Sons Limited

81 Curlew Drive, Don Mills, Ontario M3A 2R1

All Rights Reserved

Printed in the United States of America

First Edition

I am indebted to the following copyright owners for permission to reprint cartoons
owned by them:

Of the 123 drawings in this collection, 13 originally appeared in *The New Yorker,* and
were copyrighted © 1978, 1979, 1980, 1981, and 1982 by The New Yorker
Magazine, Inc.

Cartoons on pages 7, 11, 12/13, 14 top, 15, 16, 20, 21 bottom, 24, 27 top, 28,
29, 30/31, 33, 37, 41 top, 43 bottom, 45 top, 53 top, 55, 58, 60, 61, 62,
64/65, 66, 68/69, 73, 74/75, 78, 79, 83, 84/85, 87, 88, 89 top and
bottom, 91, 92, 97, 103, 106 top and bottom, 108/109, 116/117, 120, 122,
126, and 127 reprinted with permission of *National Lampoon.*

Cartoons on pages 14 bottom, 19, 21 top, 22 top, 23, 26, 27 bottom, 32, 34, 35,
39, 43 top, 48, 52, 53 bottom, 63 bottom, 67, 72, 81 bottom, 94, 99, 102,
105, 111, 112, 118, and 124 reprinted by permission: Tribune Company
Syndicate, Inc.

Cartoons on pages 17, 54, 59, 77 top and bottom, 90, 93, 107, and 110 reprinted
from *Audubon,* the magazine of the National Audubon Society.

Cartoons on pages 23 bottom, 63 top, 81 top, and 98 reprinted by permission of
Diversion magazine.

Cartoons on pages 50, 70, and 87 top are from *Woman's World.*

Cartoons on pages 51, 86, and 128 originally appeared in U.S. *Cosmopolitan.*
Reprinted with permission.

Cartoons on pages 10 and 121 © 1977 by The New York Times Company. Reprinted
by permission.

Cartoons on pages 18 and 119 first published in *Esquire,* November 1977 and
September 1977.

Cartoons on pages 41 bottom and 49 are reprinted from *Ladies' Home Journal.*

Cartoon on page 36 reprinted with permission of *Family Circle* magazine.

Cartoon on page 38 courtesy of *Texas Vision* magazine.

Cartoon on page 42 from *Intro* magazine.

Cartoon on page 82 from *HARVEY For Loving People.*

Cartoon on page 114 from *The National Enquirer.*

This book's first cartoon appears on page 7.

To the nurses in the CCU and PCU
at Lenox Hill Hospital, New York City

"It's very simple. On the Fahrenheit scale we freeze to death
at zero degrees. On the Celsius scale we freeze
to death at minus twenty degrees."

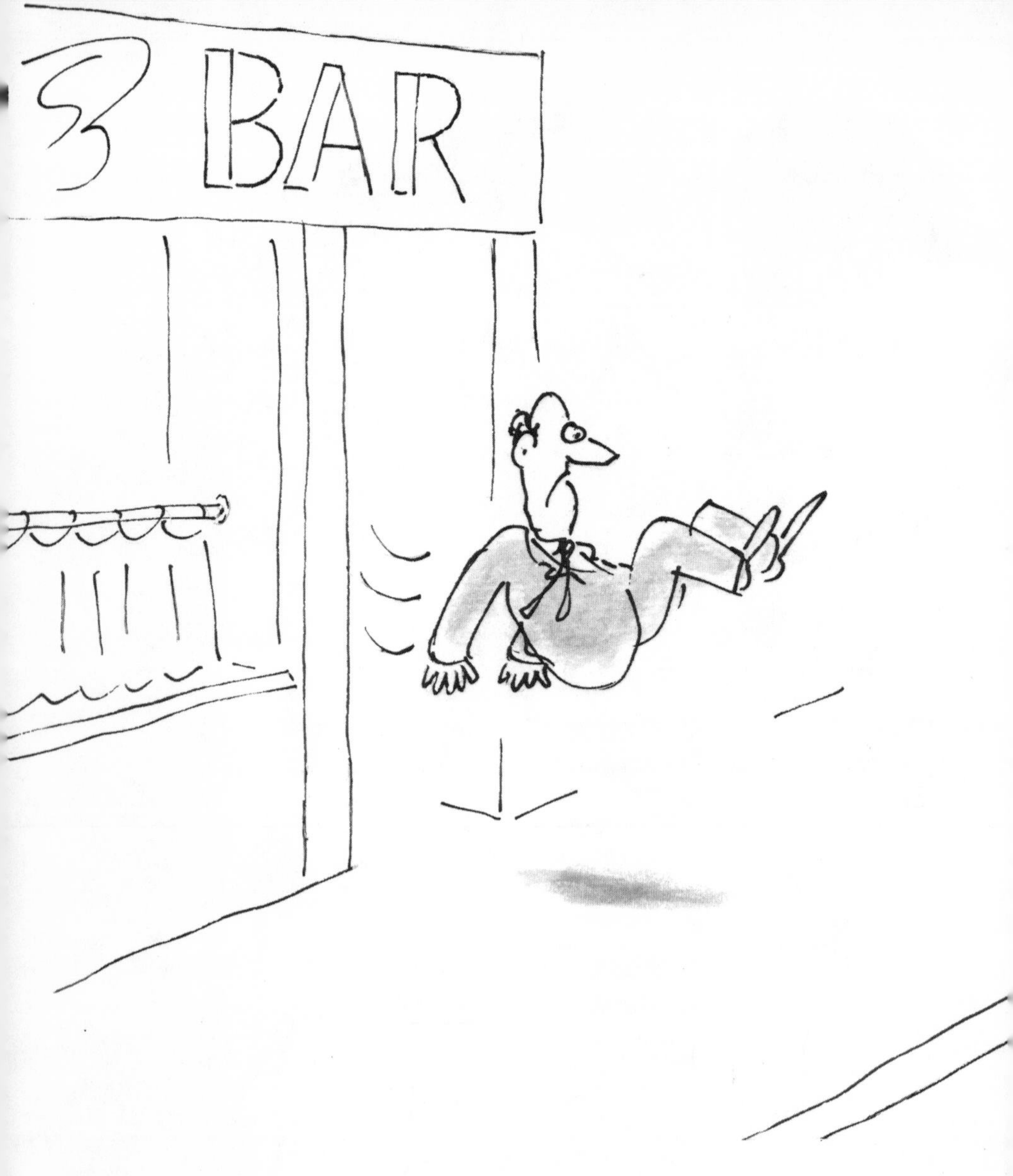
BAR

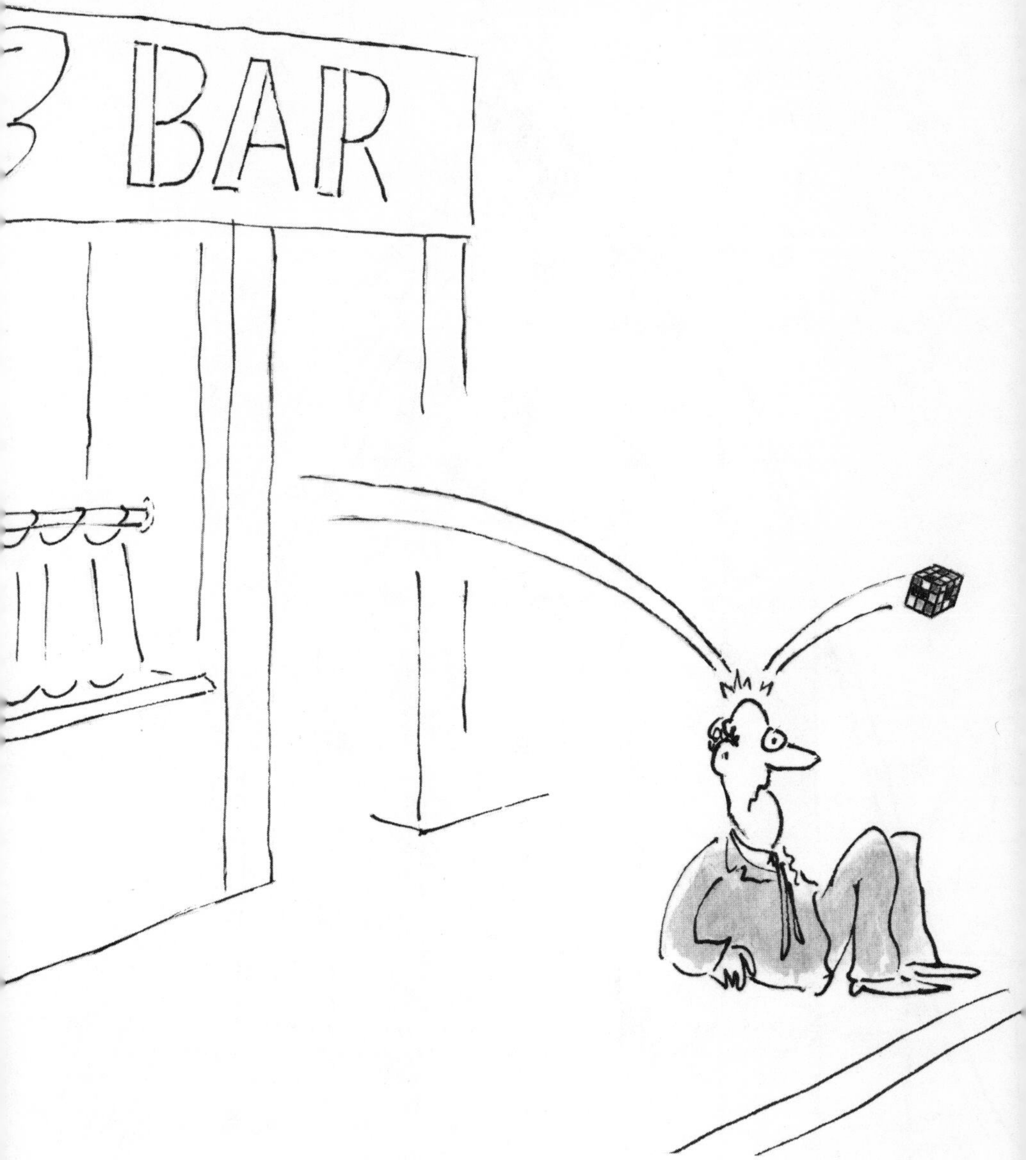
BAR

"And what did my little darling do in school today?"

"I need a day to be a vegetable."

"It tastes like salty fish."

"Darling, we can't go on meeting like th
The foundation will be finished
in a few days."

"The white one is Romulus, and the other one is Uncle Remus."

"All I can say is that I'm lucky the Red Cross was able to relocate me after the gingerbread house was destroyed."

S.GROSS

"L'état c'est moi."

"That glow; that's not radiation, is it?"

ADD YOUR OWN ADDITIVES

S. GROSS

"Damn it! You can't leave your egg
for a minute around here."

"Oh my God! I used to live he[re]"

"Okay, he now got blood in his urine. Anything else?"

"We already have cable TV."

"Get married!"

"3-in-1 oil is not much of a wish."

"The sky fell on me. Do I have a case?"

S.GROSS

"My friend Stanley says you're really a wino."

S.GROSS

"How was I supposed to know that the apple was a controlled substance

S. GROSS

"My opinion is that we ought to pull
the plug. She's a lousy lay."

eah, I know she's a crazy bitch to live with, Harry, but I need the eggs."

"Let's face it, you're through as a little match girl."

"At over $300 an ounce, you didn't expect me to keep it
unprotected in that crock, did you?"

"First of all, I don't like your sign!"

"Forget about chopping it down.
It's been declared a landmark."

"Shame on you, Mr. Watson. Another wet dream?"

"I'm sorry about ruining the pie but the other guys
down there were playing grab-ass with me."

BANK
HAPPY HOUR
2 TO 3PM
ALL CONSUMER LOANS REDUCED BY 2%
S. GROS

S. GROSS

EGGPLANT

S.GROSS

"Have you heard the news?
The tree is going co-op."

"Basically your problem is that inside of you
there's a chicken fighting to get out."

"If I hear 'Have a nice day' one more time,
I'm going to kick one of them."

"You see? God is punishing us because you bou[ght]
futures in pork bellies."

S.GROSS

THE
FIRST HOMOSEXUAL'S
BANK

NIGHT
DEPOSIT

S.GROSS

"Mein Gott! It never occurred to me that Hansel
and Gretel might be 'Hitler Youth.' "

"We've been lucky insofar that nothing
has eaten the celery."

S. GROSS

S.GROSS

"What? Not <u>another</u> identity crisis!"

"I don't know about you, but I'm giving serious thought to quitting the Klan."

"We remember Him when He was born."

"Oh for God's sake! You're making it into something bigger than it is.
It's not necrophilia if she's just sleeping."

S.GROSS

"How come you boys never call your
poor old mother any more?"

"We don't sing until we get better
working conditions."

"All I can say is the Lord works in mysterious ways."

"So <u>that's</u> why you like Swiss cheese!"

"Sir, I am the landlord and you must leave!
Dr. Jekyll doesn't have a sublet
clause in his lease."

STEROIDS
25¢

S. GROSS

"Hey kid, get lost!"

"How's that for foreplay, baby?"

S.GROSS